IA POLACCO

Sticks
and
Stones

A Paula Wiseman Book

SIMON & SCHUSTER
BOOKS FOR YOUNG READERS

New York London Toronto Sydney New Delhi

To Thom Schoff and all of those who march to the beat of a different drum

SIMON & SCHUSTER BOOKS FOR YOUNG READERS
An imprint of Simon & Schuster Children's Publishing Division
1230 Avenue of the Americas, New York, New York 10020
SIMON & SCHUSTER BOOKS FOR YOUNG READERS is a trademark of Simon & Schuster, Inc.
Certain names and characteristics have been changed.
For information about special discounts for bulk purchases, please contact Simon & Schuster Special Sales
at 1-866-506-1949 or business@simonandschuster.com.
The Simon & Schuster Speakers Bureau can bring authors to your live event.
For more information or to book an event, contact the Simon & Schuster Speakers Bureau
at 1-866-248-3049 or visit our website at www.simonspeakers.com.
Book design by Laurent Linn
The text for this book was set in Chaparral Pro.
The illustrations for this book were rendered in two and six B pencils and acetone markers.
Manufactured in China
0720 SCP
First Edition
2 4 6 8 10 9 7 5 3 1
Library of Congress Cataloging-in-Publication Data
Names: Polacco, Patricia, author, illustrator.
Title: Sticks and stones / Patricia Polacco.
Description: First edition. | New York : Simon & Schuster Books for Young Readers, Paula Wiseman Books, [2020] |
Audience: Ages 4-8. | Audience: Grades 2-3. |
Summary: When Patricia starts at a new school she quickly becomes fast friends with fellow outcasts Thom and Ravanne
and together they find a way to silence the school bully and his toadies.
Identifiers: LCCN 2019053671 (print) | LCCN 2019053672 (ebook) | ISBN 9781534426221 (hardcover) | ISBN 9781534426238 (ebook)
Subjects: CYAC: Friendship—Fiction. | Bullying—Fiction. | Individuality—Fiction. | Schools—Fiction. | Talent shows—Fiction.
Classification: LCC PZ7.P75186 Sti 2020 (print) | LCC PZ7.P75186 (ebook) | DDC [E]—dc23
LC record available at https://lccn.loc.gov/2019053671
LC ebook record available at https://lccn.loc.gov/2019053672

It was almost fall. I had spent the summer with my dad and gramma, as always, and normally I would be getting ready to fly back to California to be with my mother and go back to school. But this summer it was decided by my parents that I could stay in Michigan for the school year. I had always wanted to spend a winter with my dad, and I couldn't believe my luck! Maybe at this school I'd be popular, and no one would know that reading was so hard for me. My best summer friends, Helen and Marty, seemed to be so happy that I'd be going to school with them!

When my first day of school came, I broke out in a red rash all over my face. Of all the times to have my face full of big red blotches! Marty and Helen stopped to pick me up to walk me to school. The three of us had ridden our horses together all summer, and I felt so happy knowing that they were my good friends. But when we got to the entrance of Williamston School, they ran squealing up to a group of other girls, and then they all snubbed me. They just left me standing there all alone!

I didn't even know where my classroom was. Then a gawky-looking boy, with dark horn-rimmed glasses so thick that they made his eyes look as big as saucers, looked over my shoulder at my schedule card.

"Hey, looks like your first class is art with Mrs. Geerds! I'm going there too. I'll show you where it is," he said as he tugged at my dress. As we entered the art room, most of the tables were taken. The only one left had a very shy-looking girl sitting alone. The boy with glasses and I started to sit with her. Then a voice boomed out. "Well, looky here. Sissy boy! And who's the cootie with him?"

I looked around to see who he meant. Then I realized that he was pointing at me.

"Those are cooties on your face, aren't they?" Then all the kids laughed, and I felt my face get real hot.

"And look at who Sissy Boy and Cootie are sitting with . . . Her Ugliness," the mean boy trumpeted as he pointed at the shy girl at our table.

"The name's Thom. Not Tommy, not plain old Tom—Thom spelled with an *H*." Thom ignored the mean boy who was glowering at us. "She's Ravanne." Thom motioned to the shy girl. "We're known as Sissy Boy and Her Ugliness . . . at your service!" he chirped as he gave me a sweeping bow. "Looks like we are all in Mrs. Pederson's class together too," he added as he scanned my schedule card.

"My name's Trisha," I said. I fluttered my eyelashes. "Otherwise known as Cootie!" Then we all giggled.

"The toad's name is Billy," Thom whispered. We all crouched down and took a fleeting glance at him. He was still giving us dirty looks.

During the next days, Ravanne, Thom and I became inseparable. I found out that Ravanne designed her own textiles and painted them herself. I told them I had two loves—horses and ballet. My mom had me take ballet lessons back in California almost every day, but here in Michigan, my dad couldn't afford them. I didn't exactly know what Thom liked to do outside of school. I just knew that his mother took him somewhere on Tuesdays, Thursdays, Fridays, and some Saturdays.

I didn't know, exactly, why he was called Sissy Boy, until one day on the playground when our gym teacher asked us to form teams for a game of softball. He picked two kids to be captains, and the captains picked their teams. Even Ravanne and I got picked.

But Thom just stood there, unpicked.

"Someone pick Thom, or I'll assign him to a team!" the teacher snapped.

"Pick him, Cedrick," I whispered to our captain. "Please pick him," I added.

"Aw, all right," Cedrick said with a breathy sigh.

"But he can't play!" some of the other kids whined. "He can't even throw a ball."

As the game started I saw what they all meant. Not only did Thom strike out in the last inning and lose the game for us, but on the third swing at the ball, the bat flew out of his hands and almost hit the shortstop!

For the rest of the day, kids passed us in the hall and hissed, "Sissy Boy," at Thom. As usual, he appeared to laugh it off. But after school, Billy caught up to us as we were walking home. "I hear you lost the game. You even lost the bat!" he howled. Then he thrust his face into Thom's and bared his teeth. "Once a sissy, always a sissy." Thom had to be hurting inside, and it broke my heart.

I felt my face get real hot. "It's only a game," I blurted out. "And at least he isn't an overstuffed bully like you!" I added. "And remember sticks and stones can break bones, but names will never hurt you."

That outburst earned me a month's worth of elbow jabs in the halls from Billy and his lackeys.

The fall air was crisp and foretold the approach of winter snowfall. The winds blew in from the north. It was a Saturday, and Thom had invited Ravanne and me over to his farm. He lived in a big old farmhouse on top of a hill. It was the same farmhouse that my mom and dad had lived in when they were first married. My parents were now divorced and so were Thom's. As I walked up the steep drive, I could see him and Ravanne out in a field on the side of the house. When I caught up to them, they were both holding the most beautiful kites that I had ever seen.

"Ravanne made them!" Thom crowed as he grinned.

"I've never seen anything like these, Ravanne," I said to her.

She smiled and looked at the ground, blushing.

"She made them out of silk and hand-painted them. Here's yours," Thom said as he put the most beautiful one in my hands.

"Let's make them fly," Thom sang out as he ran, trying to catch the wind in his kite.

We all ran with our kites until they caught the wind. The kites rose, the string on our spindles making a whirring sound. When we pulled on the kites, they darted higher. When we relaxed the string, they dove and circled.

Then Thom started running across the pasture with his kite skimming the tall grass. It was almost as if he were flying.

Later, we staked the kites and lay in the tall grass and watched them soar. Ravanne hardly ever spoke, but when she did, she always said something that came from deep inside.

Cumulus clouds above rolled and made shapes that we called out to one another.

"A ship, a four-masted schooner," I called out.

"On the tossing sea," Ravanne said quietly.

"People on the deck," Thom said.

We watched that ship sail across the sky, through our glorious kites with their streamers moving like jellyfish in the sea.

"Those people? They're best friends. Just like us!" Thom said.

"I wonder where they are going?" I mused.

"Who cares, they're together. That's all that counts," Thom said as we clasped hands.

Most of the leaves of fall had fallen. Nights were getting cooler, and the scent of coming snow was in the wind. Halloween night had arrived. It was a Thursday, but Thom was home. He invited Ravanne and me over to his house to start our trick-or-treating there. He wouldn't tell us what he was going to be.

It was the first time I had ever been inside his house. I kept thinking that something should be familiar to me, but it wasn't.

"Come on!" Thom called from the top of the stairs.

Ravanne and I rushed up.

"So this is your room," I said, almost in a whisper. Since we used to live there when I was little, I wondered if it had been my room once. The walls were covered with posters from ballet companies all over the world. In his bookcase were magazines that I recognized as the kind sold at ballet performances. I picked one up.

"This is the Sadler's Wells Ballet . . . from England. I have one just like it!" I said. My mother had taken me to see the Sadler's Wells Ballet in San Francisco when I was only eight.

Thom pointed. "Look! There's Margot Fonteyn and Moira Shearer. They are the finest dancers in the world."

"Moira Shearer was in my favorite movie, *The*—" I started to say.

"*Red Shoes*!" Thom finished my sentence.

Suddenly I knew where Thom went on Tuesdays, Thursdays, Fridays, and every other Saturday.

"Do you dance, Thom? Do you take ballet?" I said as I touched his hand.

He looked intently at me for a minute. Then he leaped right into the air and pulled his toes into perfect pointes.

Ravanne smiled.

She had known all along.

I thought it was wonderful. But I wondered what Billy would do or say if he knew.

It was getting dark outside and it was time to dress for Halloween. I wore an old suit of my dad's and made up my face to look like a hobo. When Ravanne put on a flowing dress of silk she had sewn and hand-painted, I couldn't believe my eyes. When she pulled her hair back and clipped it, she was beautiful!

Then Thom walked in. He was in the middle of a wicker basket that had holes for his legs, and wrinkled clothes hanging out. "I'm dirty laundry!" he chirped, and danced across the room.

Every house we went to, people oohed and aahed over Ravanne's dress. They liked my costume too, but everyone thought Thom's was the most original and the funniest they had seen.

After we had collected as much candy as we could carry, we started home, laughing and teasing one another about who had the most candy. We were almost to Thom's when Billy and his toadies jumped out from behind Mrs. Adams's old Ford.

"Hey, look, it's Sissy Boy, Her Ugliness, and Cootie!" he sneered.

We tried to walk by him, but he blocked our way. Then he and the others grabbed our bags of candy. "Thank you, Sissy!" Billy oozed. Then he gave Thom a big shove.

Thom just stood there.

"I said, 'Thank you, Sissy.'" He shoved Thom again.

Still Thom didn't move.

I didn't know where my voice came from, but I found myself screaming at Billy. "Leave him alone, you great big bully! Pick on someone your own size!"

Billy's beady little eyes drilled holes through me. When the light flicked on on Mrs. Adams's porch, he sneered at me one last time and ran away.

I just knew that Thom was really going to be in for it now.

The Christmas holidays went by as they should. I don't think I shall ever forget the evening when Thom and his mother took Ravanne and me to see the *Nutcracker* ballet in Lansing. The four of us sat huddled together. I looked at Thom's face from time to time. His face was full of wonder when the mice were dancing and fighting the wooden soldiers, and when the sugar plum fairy danced in a line across the stage. I don't think I had ever seen pure rapture in someone's eyes until then.

In February when the valentine box was opened and valentines were handed out to every kid in class, Thom only got two—from Ravanne and me. "What?" he whispered to me. "No valentine from Billy?" He grinned. That was Thom, turning a bad situation into an okay one. How I admired him.

It was the cold winter and the whole school was abuzz about the production the school put on at the end of every year: the talent show! Just about everyone put together some sort of act: dancers, singers, yodelers, tumblers. The show was so big, even parents came.

Ravanne, Thom, and I weren't sure if we would be in the show or not. If we wanted to be. But we liked to sit in the bleachers in the gym after school and watch the other kids practice. Thom always had something encouraging to say to almost every kid that performed.

"Good job, Cheryl," he said after she tap-danced.

"Hey, Danny, you nailed that balance beam."

One day after rehearsal, we were in our usual place in the gym when the coach set up bars for the track team to practice the high jump. Billy was the captain, and his main claim to fame was the high jump.

But after he cleared the 5'3" mark up to the 5'9" mark, we watched him make runs at the bar and miss again and again.

"Billy," the coach said, "you have to nail this. This team has a chance at the state finals. It's only a quarter of an inch more. I'm asking you!" The coach seemed annoyed.

Billy tried again and missed. I could see Thom watching.

When practice was over, Thom, Ravanne, and I climbed down to the gym floor.

Then, all of a sudden, Thom took a run at the high bar! And leaped over it with six inches to spare. He was in a complete split as he sailed over the bar.

"See what ballet can do for you!" Thom sang out as he landed.

It was then that we realized that Billy and the coach had not left the room. They both heard what Thom had said.

"Ballet? Ballet or not, kid, why haven't you tried out for the team?" the coach asked. Billy's fists were white from squeezing so hard.

Thom's face was red. "I was just fooling around," he stammered. He grabbed his book bag and made for the door. The coach kept trying to call after him, but Thom didn't turn back.

We were almost home when Billy suddenly straddled the sidewalk in front of us. He was alone this time. He jumped Thom and pushed him to the ground so hard that his glasses flew off.

"My glasses. . . . I can't see without my glasses!" Thom pleaded.

Billy picked them up and held them in front of his face. "You mean these, you little priss? You little butterfly ballet dancer," Billy said in a mocking, whiny voice. "Wait until I tell everyone at school."

"Please, my glasses. I need them!" Thom begged him. "They're the only ones I have!"

With that, Billy dropped them and stepped on them, grinding them into the ground. Then he laughed and ran away.

For the first time, I saw Thom cry. He sat down on the curb, and tears ran down his face. "Mom won't be able to get me new glasses for a long time. She just can't. They're so expensive!"

Ravanne and I sat with Thom between us, not knowing what to say.

Suddenly his face changed. I didn't realize how handsome he was without his glasses. He had beautiful dark eyes.

"I'm going to be in the talent show!" Thom said with real resolve.

"Will you dance, Thom?" I asked.

Thom wiped tears out of his eyes. "Yes," he said. "Yes. I am going to dance."

As the days passed Thom practiced and practiced a dance he had danced in a performance the year before. Thom's mother had taped his glasses but he couldn't dance in them very well. So Ravanne and I helped him block out the space on the stage, because he couldn't see well enough to be sure where he was stepping.

When the big day arrived, Ravanne helped him into his costume in a closet so that no one would see him until he stepped onstage. I stood just in front of the stage on the gym floor so I could warn him in case he came too close to the edge. I gave the record to the person who was going to turn on the phonograph for Thom's dance.

Finally, there was a hush. The annual spring program commenced with Freeda Harding's tap dance. Then Jesse DeWitt did bird calls. The Girls' Glee Club sang three selections from *Oklahoma*. The principal made a boring speech, which was followed by two really dumb skits by the Boys' Athletic Club. Then, just before Thom, the pompom girls did a routine they called Razzle Dazzle.

Then it was time.

Thom was on!

The empty stage was dimly lit except for one spotlight in the middle of the backdrop. Ravanne cued the music. First they missed the track and there was a loud scratching sound. Then a melody from the ballet *Swan Lake* echoed from the wings.

Thom stepped into the spotlight. He was dressed all in white, in the classic costume of Prince Siegfried from *Swan Lake*. He seemed to be glowing.

Then Billy jumped up on his seat and called out, "It's Sissy Boy!" A girl shrieked, and then some boys gave catcalls, and finally laughter resounded as what seemed like hundreds of students stomped their feet on the gym floor.

Thom began to dance anyway. The laughter was so loud that the record could hardly be heard. But Thom danced. Perfect pirouettes, spinning like a top. He was so graceful, so elegant. He was the swan prince. Someone reached in and took off the music, but Thom didn't stop. He didn't even need the music. His leaps were high and powerful. Athletic! At times, he looked as if he were suspended on a wire. Thom kept dancing.

The catcalls and the laughter and jeering started to die down. Thom kept dancing. He leaped and turned, making sweeping steps across the stage. Finally there was complete silence. All that could be heard was the shuffle and thumps of Thom's feet landing on the wooden stage.

Then, before it was even over, there was the sound of a single person clapping, then another and another! The room exploded. The thunder of the clapping moved in one huge wave toward the stage.

Thom finished his dance with a grand leap, landing in the center of the stage. Then he bowed. One by one, kids rose to their feet clapping and cheering. Soon the entire auditorium was standing. The sound of their whistles and cheers was deafening.

Thom received a standing ovation that lasted a full four minutes. I counted.

When I gave him his glasses his mother had taped together, tears rolled down my face.

"Thom, I've never seen something so brave in my life," I sobbed. "I was so worried when you said you were going to dance today. But you showed them. You showed them! And they loved you too."

No one ever laughed at him again, and the only name they knew him by was Thom.
Not Tommy or Tom. T-h-o-m Thom.

I returned to California after that summer and resumed my schooling and my own ballet classes there. Every summer when I returned to Williamston to see Dad, I always made time to see Thom and Ravanne. And they made time for me.

The last the three of us were together was the summer of our eighteenth birthdays. At the end of that summer, just before I left, we all stood on that windy hill above Thom's house. I was set to go to art school in the fall—it turned out I did that better than ballet. Ravanne was going to apprentice with a dressmaker in Chicago. Thom had been accepted to a New York ballet school. We clasped hands. We didn't say anything. There was no need to. We knew that moment would be in our hearts as long as we lived.

Author's Note

Dear readers,

It's hard to believe that Thom's dance was over fifty years ago. He still lives in New York City and is now retired as the artistic director of the American School of Ballet. Ravanne lives in Paris and is retired after an incredible career as a fashion designer.

As for Billy? I just hope that he outgrew being a bully because there is no place in a kind world for bullies.

Ah, then there's me. Well, you already know what I do. I make books just for you. I'm grateful that I can, and I'm grateful for Thom and his story. It pleases me that you will know him now.

Oh, and one more thing. If you are the kind of kid who marches to a different drum like Ravanne, Thom, and me, step high! Strut your stuff with courage and goodwill. That cadence will take you to places that your heart aches for and where your dreams dare to lead you. Your heart knows the way!

Patricia Polacco